THE
Muddy Foot Prince

WRITTEN BY

Alicia Hogan Murphy

ILLUSTRATED BY

Michael Schweitzer

CURLY PRESS

Books to Curl Up With

For John, Colleen, and Brendan...
your footprints are growing bigger every day, just like my love for you!
And for Jack, who always leaves his shoes under the island...
at least they aren't muddy. xoxo
—ALICIA HOGAN MURPHY

This book is dedicated to
my queen, Lisa, and my princes, Xavier and Zeke.
—MICHAEL SCHWEITZER

Published by CurlyQPress
Mansfield, Massachusetts
www.CurlyQPress.com

© 2015 Alicia Hogan Murphy
Illustrations by Michael Schweitzer

ISBN: 978-1-941216-08-8
E-ISBN: 978-1-941216-09-5

Library of Congress Control Number: 2014957999

PRINTED IN CHINA

Prince Oliver James Huntington IV had ruined thirty-seven pairs of black, shiny-buckled dress shoes. Not just with a little scuff or slight splatter of mud—he'd gotten them filthy!

The palace where Prince Oliver lived stood at the top of a tall hill, looking over the entire kingdom. At the bottom of that tall hill was a beautiful pond where the prince spent his days looking for frogs, catching snakes, and chasing butterflies.

Prince Oliver loved to dig for worms, fish for fish, and make mud pies. At the end of the day, he would race back to the palace to share his discoveries with his parents, King Oliver James Huntington III and Queen Mildred Rose Huntington.

Ordering him to leave his pond friends outside, the king and queen would yell at Prince Oliver for getting the palace floor dirty with his muddy, wet shoes.

"Princes *don't* play in ponds!" the king would yell.

"Nor do they play with frogs and snakes or make mud pies!" the queen would add.

"But I like to do all of those things. It's fun," the prince would explain. "Besides, I have no one else to play with—I get lonely. So I make friends with the animals."

"But you ruin your good shoes each day, and we have to send for new ones!" the queen argued.

"You have so many toys in your royal bedroom. Why don't you play there?" suggested the king one day.

"It's not as much fun," the prince said. "Outside, I can be with nature. I can see how it looks, enjoy how it smells, and hear how it sounds."

The king and queen
shook their heads.

One day, after discovering a small log full of beeswax, the prince, so excited, came running through the grand front hallway in his freshly ruined, muddy shoes. He slipped on the shiny marble floor, wet from washing, and dropped the log, which broke and made a gooey mess.

"Prince Oliver James Huntington IV!" shouted Queen Mildred Rose Huntington. "What have you done? You made a terrible mess on the marble floor! And you ruined your shoes again!"

"I'm sorry," he mumbled.

Sorry isn't good enough anymore!" yelled the king.
"From now on, you are not to play down by the pond.
Now clean up this mess at once!" The king and queen
stormed out of the grand front hallway.

Prince Oliver looked at his broken log dripping with sticky honey and bits of beeswax on the not-so-shiny marble floor. His eyes filled with tears as he said, "I didn't mean to ruin the nice shiny floor, or my shoes. I just wanted to show everyone my log."

That night, the prince lay awake in his bed. "No one understands me here," he said to the darkness. "The palace would be a much quieter and cleaner place if I just left."

He made his bed, packed a small bag, and crept quietly down the grand staircase and through the front hallway. He sneaked past the guard at the main gate and left the palace without anyone knowing.

Prince Oliver ran down to the pond to say good-bye to his animal friends. But where were the croaking frogs and slithering snakes? The water was quiet and still. Where were the jumping fish and tiny turtles?

"Whooo! Whooo!" cried a voice suddenly. Prince Oliver James Huntington IV gasped. He looked around but saw no one. It was awfully dark. "Who's there?" his shaky voice called.

Only silence answered. The prince felt a chill run down his back. He'd forgotten to pack a warm sweater. His shoes sank slightly into the mud beside the pond. He thought about starting down the road into the village but shivered with fear. He'd never been away from the palace at night before.

"Maybe I'll run away in the morning, after it gets light," Prince Oliver said to himself. "I'll sleep in the warm carriage house. It won't be so dark and cold after the sun comes up."

He trudged back up the hill. The carriage house wasn't as cozy as his own bedroom, but the prince found a warm corner where he curled up and was soon fast asleep.

Queen Mildred Rose Huntington awoke at the crack of dawn.
Coming out of her royal bedroom, she saw sunlight beaming
into the hallway from her son's room. Peeking in, she saw that
Prince Oliver's bed was empty and hadn't been slept in!

The queen ran down the grand staircase and looked downstairs for her son. He was nowhere to be found. She awakened the king and alerted everyone in the palace that the prince was missing.

When he wasn't found anywhere in the palace, the king and queen asked their driver to take them to search the village. They were headed down the road toward the main gate when suddenly the queen cried, "Stop!"

"What is it?" asked the king.

"Look," said Queen Mildred, pointing to the walkway near the carriage house. "Muddy footprints."

They burst into the
carriage house and found
Prince Oliver, still sleeping
soundly. The queen ran to
him and scooped him into
her arms. Prince Oliver was
startled when he saw his
parents.

"I know you're angry with me," the prince said. "I was
trying to make things right by leaving. I know I should be
happy playing with my toys, and I should not mess up the
palace. But I love to go outside and fish, look for snakes,
catch frogs, and play by the pond. I'm sorry—I hope you
can still love me."

The king looked at the queen with a tear in his eye. "We're sorry, too," he said. "We were wrong to get so mad. It's just mud—it's not really that important."

"I'll try not to cause any more trouble," said the prince.

"You're no trouble at all," smiled the queen, hugging her son again. "Thank goodness for your muddy footprints—they helped us find you!"

Later that day, the king looked out the window and had an idea. "Why don't we build you a greenhouse on the hill, where you can grow plants and keep your frogs and snakes?"

"Really?" the prince grinned. "Wow!
Would you help me with the planting?"
"We'd love to," smiled the queen.

In the end, the king and queen had learned a lesson about what truly matters. And Prince Oliver James Huntington IV learned that it is okay to be messy sometimes…in the *right* place!

THE END